ROBOTS VS PRINCESSES VS UNICORNS VS HAMSTERS

by Chris White

Design by Robot Zillamog.

First published by Mogzilla in 2015.

ISBN: 978-1-906132-90-3

Once upon a Wednesday, in a galaxy just round the corner, there lived a very specia unicorn.

Of course all unicorns are special because they are magical and can poop RAINBOWS But this unicorn was extra special. Her name was Sasha, and Sasha was a Space Unicorn!

Sasha lived a really happy life on the The Planet of the Space Unicorns. The planet was full of unicorns who danced and clip-clopped and polished each other's unicorn horns.

Sasha was very proud of her horn as it was the longest and pointiest on the whole planet.

Nothing bad ever happened on The Planet of the Unicorns. Until yesterday...
Yesterday it was blown into smithereens!!

BANG

Sasha was very lucky though. She escaped. She had just popped for a gallop to the shops for some scrummy cake and fizzy pop when...

WHOOOOSH! BANG! BOOOOM!

Her planet had been blown into a gazillion tiny pieces.

She stared at what used to be the place she called home and shed a shiny unicorn tear.

Where was she going to dance and clip-clop now? She shed another tear and ran off into space, feeling very down.

She would have to find somewhere else to live now. Hopefully somewhere with scrummy cake and fizzy pop.

Just a few space miles away is another planet. Shhhh. Listen carefully...

"ZZZZZ! Squeak!
"ZZZZ! Squeak..."

Yes, The Planet of the Hamsters is the sleepiest, snuggliest planet in the whole universe. The hamsters just lie about all day long. Sleeping, scratching, snuffling and sometimes counting sunflower seeds to check if they have enough food. They always do.

It is the most peaceful and calm planet around.

Nobody would ever
want to
BLOW IT UP!!!

Let's **BLOW UP** the Planet of the Hamsters!!!" boomed a voice.

The voice belonged to Robo 614, the robot in charge of The Remarkable Robo Ray Gun.
"Errr, why?" asked Robo 420, his assistant, "What have they ever done to us Sir?"
"I just don't trust them," Robo 614 sneered in his robotic voice. "They're just too fluffy!"
There was no place for being different on The Planet of the Robots. That included being 'fluffy'.
"We can't just blow them up for no reason Sir..."
Robo 614 was very frustrated because he hadn't blown anything up for a long time.
Then, as luck would have it, that horrible fluffy planet had floated into view. His eyes flashed red...
"I'm watching you, you fluffy freaks..."

Nibbles the hamster yawned.
"What was that noise?" he thought.
He looked over at all the other hamsters snoozing in their fluffy beds.
He flopped out of his pile of fluff, scratched his head and a half-eaten sunflower seed fell out of his ear onto the ground.
Nibbles scampered up the ladder to the planet's fluffy surface. He popped his head out and glanced over the fluffy landscape. There stood a purple unicorn.
Nibbles had never seen a unicorn before, never mind a purple one. He was a bit startled.
"Hi!" said Sasha.
"Hi!" said Nibbles, "Do you want to come and snuggle?"
Sasha wasn't really sure what snuggling was. Unicorns didn't snuggle in case they poked each in the eye with their horns.

"Let's snuggle!" Sasha laughed. And she leapt down the hole.

Later, after a snuggling session,
Nibbles was giving
Sasha a tour.
"What's that?"
asked Sasha.

"That's some fluff..." said Nibbles.
"NO..." Sasha pointed with her hoof towards the huge deadly weapon next to a pile of sunflower seeds,
"WHAT'S THAT?"
"Oh, that? That is our planet's defence system. You'll never guess what it fires."
"Sunflower seeds?" guessed Sasha, confidently.
"Oh, you're clever!" squeaked Nibbles.
"What's it for?"
"Protection."
"Against what?"
"Y'know. Things. And stuff. We've never actually fired it. I just know that it is a Super Seed Shooter 6000 and it could destroy a planet."
Sasha remembered how her planet had been destroyed and cried another unicorn tear.
She turned to Nibbles for a comforting cuddle. But Nibbles was face down in a fluff pile, fast asleep.

A few space miles away is another planet spinning in the sky. It is sparkly like a floating disco ball. This is The Planet of the Princesses. Look! There is Princess Girly talking to Princess Pinky Pinkerton. I bet they are chatting about shopping or jewellery or ponies.

Let's listen in to their conversation...
"Good work on blasting that planet, Princess!"
"Thank you Princess. It was a terrific shot wasn't it?!"
"Tee Hee! Tremendous fun too! Let's find another planet to blow up with our Dastardly Diamond Destroyer this afternoon!"
"Yes! Yes! Then we will have lemonade and chocolate cupcakes!"
All the princesses giggled and clapped their hands. WHAT?!?
Yes, that's right. It turns out that these princesses are the nastiest,
evilest beings in the universe! They were the ones who blasted The Planet of the Unicorns to bits with their Dastardly Diamond Destroyer!
Bad princesses!
"Tee Hee Hee!" they all giggled, evilly.

Sasha was ready to go back and snuggle for a while. She took one last look at the Super Seed Shooter 6000 and thought that she had seen enough of nasty weapons and destruction.

"I don't want to see anything destroyed ever again, "she whispered to herself.

It was then that a small piece of fluff floated up Sasha's nose.

"Ah...ah...AH...AHTCHOOOOOOOOOOO!"

The sleeping Nibbles shot off her back, flew through the air and landed right on the large red button that said "FIRE".

A stream of sunflower seeds shot out of the massive gun and happened to hit The Planet of the Princesses!

KABOOOOOOM!

"Oops!" said Sasha.

Nibbles opened one eye, "What did I miss?"

"Ummmmm," Sasha mumbled, "It's not what you missed, but what you hit..."

FIRE

PZZZ!
614
420

Robo 614 looked at Robo 420 and bleeped:
"Did you just see that?!"
They both stared at the screen in front of them.
"THOSE FLUFFY FIENDS!" said Robo 420. His moustache fell off with shock.
"This is the excuse we've been looking for! Let's fry the fluffy freaks! LET'S BLOW UP THE PLANET OF THE HAMSTERS!"
The Remarkable Robo Ray Gun swung into action with a loud "PZZZ! BOOM! WHAPOOOOOR!" and a bright red laser ray shot through space towards the fluffy ball in the distance. The Planet of the Hamsters exploded into a million bits of fluff and seed.
Robo 420 found his moustache and both robots looked smugly at the scene of destruction on the screen.
"Lovely. Fancy a nice cup of oil Sir..?"

PP1

Speeding through the stars came
Pink Petal 1, the princess's spaceship.
Luckily they had seen the sunflower seeds
heading towards their planet just in time.
They grabbed their handbags and jumped
on-board. No princess was left behind.
Princess Moonbeam squealed,
"Let's go to The Planet of the Robots!
They just blew up The Planet of the
Hamsters didn't they?"
All the princesses nodded. Some crowns
fell off.
"We'll get along just fine with them. I
like their style!"
"YES! YES!!" the princesses squealed.
"And if we don't get along...we'll blast
them!" Princess Starlight yelled.
Soon their ship touched down on the
metal surface of The Planet of the
Robots. They did get along really well and
they had a big party to celebrate.
The robots enjoyed drinking lemonade as
they had never tried it. The princesses
didn't like drinking oil though.

ZOOOOOOM!
What's that?!
It's Sasha the Space Unicorn!
But wait. What's that on her back?
HOORAY! It's the entire population of
The Planet of the Hamsters!
Sasha has flown them all to safety!
No hamster was left behind!
WHOOP!
"Where do we go now?" Sasha yelled to the massive mound of hamsters on her back, "I've already been on two planets that have exploded. I don't want to go through that again."
"Why don't we head down there?" squeaked Chubby the Hamster.
Sasha pointed her horn in the direction of The Planet of the Robots and began to gallop through the stars.
"It should be safe, I suppose," Sasha chuckled to herself, "I think I've seen the last of any exploding planets for a while!"
Just then, another planet exploded.

Hang on... This is getting silly! What just happened?!!

Well, Robo 614 was showing Princess Pinky the Remarkable Robo Ray Gun. Princess Pinky leaned over to see where the Hyper-Galactic Boom Boom Gubbin plugged into the Flux-Wiggle Thingamabob and her crown wobbled off.

It went tink, clank, tink, clank all the way down into its workings.

The Remarkable Robo Ray Gun began to whir and whine then smoke started to fill the room.

Then an alarm went 'BEEEEEEP! BOOOOOOP!'

Then a robotic voice went, "WARNING! RAY GUN WILL EXPLODE IN 10...9...8..."

Then a room full of robots and princesses went "AAARRRGGGH!!!"

Everybody ran into the Rockin' Robo Rocket Ship to escape.

3...2...1...BANG!!!!

The Rockin' Robo Rocket Ship blasted away from the bits of metal that once was The Planet of the Robots.

If the Robots (or the Princesses) had switched on the headlights, then they would have seen a space unicorn (with hundreds of hamsters on her back) galloping straight towards their ship.

But they didn't see Sasha. And Sasha didn't see the Robot's ship.

The unicorn's unbreakable horn went 'PRANG!' straight into the Rockin' Robo Rocket Ship's Robo Thruster 3000. Steam began to twirl out of the hole and warning lights flashed.

"Oops!" said Sasha, "Sorry!"

The hamsters said nothing as they were all asleep.

Now, as everybody knows, a Robo Thruster 3000 is vital to a Rockin' Robo Rocket Ship's movement.

Without one, it can't move at all.

"We're stuck!" yelled Robo 123.
"Where will we get fizzy lemonade?" squealed Princess Flutterby.
"HOW CAN WE GO SHOPPING?!?!?" screamed Princess Pinky.

Suddenly the ship lurched forwards!
"What's going on?" Robo 333 asked.
"Help!" squealed Princess Squealy.
Everybody ran to the window and saw an incredible sight! The hamsters had made a long line by linking paws.
At the end of the line was Nibbles hanging onto Sasha's tail.
Sasha was galloping forwards with all her might. They were towing the broken ship through space.

"We'll have to head to that planet over there. It's the only place around here that's still in one piece!"
It was true. They had nearly run out of planets to live on.

The robots and the hamsters and the princesses and the unicorn all agreed they would all be friends and live on this new planet together.

They promised to all get along and not blow it up. They couldn't afford to. There was nowhere else to go. They had to show the only planet they'd got some love.

So they all lived there happily ever after. Tolerating and respecting each other.
It was a place full of oil and fizzy lemonade and sunflower seeds and RAINBOW poop.

And they called their new home...

THE
PLANET OF THE
ROBO-PRINCESS-UNI-HAMSTERS!

MOGZILLA

Lightning Source UK Ltd.
Milton Keynes UK
UKIC01n2037140715
255208UK00002B/6
* 9 7 8 1 9 0 6 1 3 2 9 0 3 *